THE
BAD SOUL
SERIES

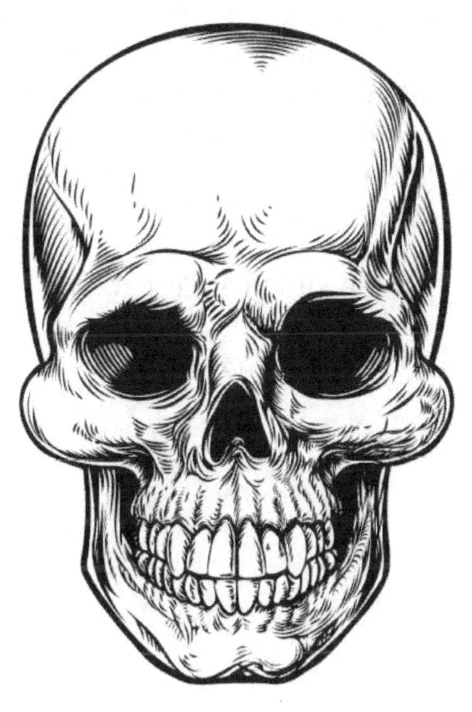

MARYFICS

First edition Augest 2022
Book Design by Ayyaz Khan
Published By Ayyaz khan Publishing

Part 1

You and Jungkook shifted to your new house due to violence in city. You both wanted an area which could be peaceful rather than being noisy a lot even at nights.

The area around your house was BREATHTAKING. Tall and wide trees going along with the road but the calmness there was too much. It seemed like only you both are going to live in that area. Because the houses were far from each other. Other than this, the place, the area and also your house was just like you both wanted it to be.

When you both arrived at your place, you couldn't believe what you were seeing. A big, a very big house (not a mansion) along with a beautiful lawn which was spreaded across your whole house. There was also a big garage where, at a time, three or four cars could be parked each side. A gap was formed in between your lips, you couldn't even believe what you actually saw. Jungkook chuckled after seeing your reaction.

" Close your mouth baby. There might be many flies wanting to dance in your mouth. " You playfully glared at him but laughed along after. " Seriously kook this place is just... amazing. " Not helping with yourself, you immediately ran to the front door of the house, already excited to explore the inside. By seeing your desperate self, Jungkook immediately but happily gave you the house keys to open the front door. He only wanted YOUR'S steps first in the house.

Happily you opened the door but stopped right away after seeing what was in front of your eyes. A wide living room with wide stairs in the mid of the room leading the person to the second floor. Your mouth again made

a gap but this time, it was bigger than before. " omg......
Jungkook... OH MY GODDDD THIS HOUSE IS SOOOO
BEAUTIFUL. I'm feeling like I have entered in a palace.
" you said. "You liked this baby? " he asked you. "Liked
this?? I LOVED THIS. I'm totally in love with this house. "
you squealed in happiness. "That's not fair baby. You can
only love meee. " he immediately pouted at your happy
comment. "Aww.. don't worry baby, the only person I
love in this world is YOU. And no one can change that!
Thank you soo much for this house. Its really beautiful."
you said in love making Jungkook happy.

"Do you want to see our room?" he asked. "Is that
a question? Come on let's go." You pulled him with you
but stopped right at the top of stairs because there were
so many rooms and you didn't even know which one was
yours. Jungkook then chuckled and pulled you towards
left and at the end of the hallway, there was a big door.
"Open it baby." he told you.

Nervously but happily you opened the door and you
knew that at first sight, you fell in love with this massive
room who has a king sized bed in mid along with a
wide attached bathroom. Headwall behind the bed was
furnished with a red color wallpaper and one wall was
like glass wall because on the other side, there was a
big balcony. You turned to Jungkook and immediately
hugged him.

"Seriously kook, you didn't have to buy such a big
house." you truly said burying your head in the crook
of his neck."But you loved it, right?" "Of course, I loved
it. Thank you so much kook. " you broke the hug and
kissed his cheek. "Hey... you don't have to thank me. You
are my wife (basically you both are married) amd I will
do anything for you." At this time, you couldn't believe
how you got so much lucky to have him. He hugged you

once again. After the hug, you both decided to bring and set the small things like decoration pieces, books, etc. After an hour of decorating the things, you both got hungry. Then you both decided to order something. After oredering the food, Jungkook went to take a shower while you decided to explore the remaining house.

By the time, when you were done with the exploration, you were happily going back to your both shared room. While passing through the hallway on ground floor, you heard a screeching sound like someone was opening the door but very slowly. You turned around and saw to your right. There was a door which you thought you hadn't explored yet. The door was actually opening by itself. But what scared you a little was that you felt like someone was watching you through the space inside the door but you couldn't see because inside was totally dark. You took slow steps towards the door and fully opened the remaining door. You pressed the light buttons and the lights of the room turned on. But it wasn't a room, there were stairs inside which you thought lead towards the basement. You peeked down a little but couldn't see through darkness. You went to living room, took the torch from the table and again went towards the basement room. You turned on the torch, then went downstairs. What you saw surprised you a little. There was a whole bunch of old and rough furniture which seemed to belong to the family which you didn't even know when used to live here. The basement was actually covered with layers of dust. You were thinking of going upwards but when you turned around, there came a sound which you thought of a piano. It was like someone just pressed a piano key. You turned back again and saw a piano in front of you. It was covered with a lot of durt. You went towards it and randomly pressed a key but the sound didn't came. You then pressed on some other keys. By the time,

You were getting scared because no sound was coming from any key you pressed. You were frozen due to shock and fear. Your mind was neither functioning well nor understanding what was actually happening. You were 100% sure that the sound you heard was actually of the piano. But it wasn't functioning under your touch.

Suddenly the door bell rang throughout the whole house bringing you back to your senses. You immediately ran upstairs because you were not feeling well there.

The feeling you were getting was sickening you. You were going to open the door but someone suddenly put its hand on your shoulder.

Part 2

You were shocked to death. You suddenly screamed and turned around only to find Jungkook staring worriedly at you. "HUH.. OMG Jungkook you scared the hell out of me. " you said and put your hand on your chest feeling your increased heartbeat. "Sorry baby I didn't mean to scare you. Just go sit on the couch I will bring the food! " he said pushing you towards the couch and opening the door to receive food from the delivery guy.

He brought the food to the couch and sat down beside you. You both began to eat the food. During munching the food, you told Jungkook about the basement, but didn't tell him about the piano incident. He decided to see it after eating. By the time you both finished the food, you brought plates to the sink while Jungkook went to the basement with a torch. When he reached downstairs, he was shocked to hell.

"Holly Shit... What's all this? " He was shocked to see all the furniture. He saw a light socket hanging down the ceiling. He immediately brought a light bulb and fixed it into the socket. After that he turned on the light. Basement brightened with the light bulb. He saw each and everything, also the piano. He also found some useful things which could be used later. He decided to go back but when he turned around he stepped on something. He looked down to see his foot on a doll's head. He picked up the doll but made a disgusting face by looking at the weird-scary looking doll. He put it on the piano table then headed upstairs and closed the door of the basement.

By the time, you were done washing the dishes and cleaning the kitchen. Jungkook came towards you and gave you a back hug then kissed your neck softly.

"Let's sleep baby. I'm super tired. " he murmured in your neck which gave you a ticklish feeling making you giggle. "But kook its only 7:30 pm." you told him. He groaned and said, "Aw come on baby, I'm tired. " "Okay, but did you check the basement? "you asked him in curiosity. "Yeah its too big. We can keep a lot of things and extra furniture in it. What do you say?" "Yeah, you're right. Okay done. Let's go to sleep."

You both headed to your shared bedroom. Before going to sleep, you took a warm shower because it was a lot cold due to foresty area. When you were done having the shower, you wore a black hoddie and some baggy trousers for comfort. When you laid down beside Jungkook, he immediately took you in his warm embrace and held you tightly. He kissed your forehead multiple times and you both said to each other a goodnight and slept.

You both were sleeping in each other's embrace, but suddenly, you saw in your dream that someone was following you. You sped up but the person was fast enough to catch you. He held your arm, turned you around and said, "Stay away from her. She is very dangerous." You were scared but confused and asked him who. "Leave the house, if you don't then you both will die. " You were now scared to death and asked him again and again that who's the female he's talking about. But suddenly the person's facial expressions changed to feared ones. He tried to run away but someone stabbed him right in his head.

You immediately woke up and sat up on the bed. Your heart was beating faster and sweat was dripping from your forehead. You turned to your side table and picked the water bottle. You gulped down the whole bottle due to shock and tried to balance your breath by taking deep breaths. You turned to your left to see Jungkook sleeping peacefully. You sighed "What a nightmare! "and decided to sleep again. You laid down and closed your eyes but suddenly, you heard a noise coming from downstairs. You immediately sat up and tried to understand the sound. It was like a muffled sound which you couldn't process clearly. You wore your shoes and headed to your room door. You opened the door and the sound become a little but not completely clear. You went towards the stairs and peeked down a little to the right side.

The sound was coming through the hallway downstairs. You slowly but in fear went downstairs and turned on the living room light. You went towards the hallway and tried to hear the sound from where it was coming. When you passed the basement door, the sound became a little muffled.

You turned to your left and again heard the sound. It was coming from the basement. Now you were sure you were neither hallucinating nor having a dream. With the shaking hands, you opened the door and turned on the light.

Now the sound was clear enough to be heard but what you heard was like someone was singing along the music. The music was of the pianos. You didn't know that Jungkook had fixed the basement's light that's why you held the torch. You turned it on and held it towards the piano from upstairs. You saw that a weird looking lady was sitting on the seat and playing the piano. You were shocked to death to see an unexpected lady singing and playing the piano in your house's basement when you knew that there is no one except you and your husband in this house. You went a little down and now you were standing in the middle of the stairs. Your hands were shaking and your voice was like stuck in your throat.

But in the shock, you asked "w-w-Who are you?... " The lady stopped singing but remained in her position. Her back was facing you. "He told you to leave the house right! " Her spooky and hoarse voice came like a whisper but you heard it. Now you couldn't believe which one was a dream, this one or the one you saw before. But then she slowly started turning her head around. But half of the way, your torch turned off itself. Your breath hitched and you tried to turn it on but it wasn't turning on. After so many tries, it turned on. You immediately held it towards the piano but now the lady wasn't there anymore. You saw everywhere with the help of torch but she was nowhere to be found.

You were in too much shock that you immediately began to run upstairs but someone held your ankle to not let you go.

Part 3

Someone tried to pull you downwards. You began to scream uncontrollably and tried to free your ankle. Luckily you got it free and immediately ran towards your shared bedroom. You were screaming all the way to your bedroom due to heavy shock. Jungkook woke up after hearing someone screaming. He looked to your side but you were not there. Suddenly you barged into the room in a wrecked state, hair messy and tears all over your face.

Jungkook's eyes widened after seeing you like this, he immediately stood up from the bed and you ran towards him and hugged him tightly. You were crying badly as well as shaking uncontrollably. He got really worried. "Hey.. Y/n, what happened? Baby why are you crying? Tell me. "he was getting more worried about your state. "s-s-som-some-someone 'hiccup'.... s-s-som... " you couldn't even speak clearly. Jungkook brought you to bed and sat you down then hugged you tightly and began to rub your back to sooth your cries a little. He spoke sweet words to comfort you through your anxiety.

After what seemed like infinity, you calmed down a little but were still sniffing. Jungkook broke the hug, cupped your cheeks and made you look towards him. "Honey, what happened? Why were you screaming? You know I will always be there for you hun. " Even thinking about the incident made you shake a little but in Jungkook's embrace, you felt safe a lot. "Th-there was someone, a-a l-lady, playing piano in the basement. But then, m-my torch turned off itself. When I turned it on, sh-she was not there anymore, kook..... She was gone. I-I tried looking for her but she wasn't there. " At this point, you broke down in tears again. Jungkook hugged your figure again and said;

"Baby, there's no one except us in here. You must took it wrong.. Y/n.. you must be hallucinating. " You broke the hug and looked him in the eyes in disbelief, "NO JUNGKOOK... Its not my hallucination, she was there. I saw her with my own eyes. Sh-she was there playing the pian_" "Baby... you must be tired. Kitten you should take a rest. Okay? Let's talk about this tomorrow, hmm? " You gave in thinking that you must got it wrong. He laid you down in between his arms and began stroking your hair to ease your mind. He started singing DECALCOMANIA for you. His angelic yet sweet voice calmed you down amd made you sleepy. In no time, you were fast asleep in his arms. He was looking at your peaceful face, then kissed your forehead and lips softly a multiple times then joined you in your sleep.

Next day you woke up from the sunlight directly hitting your face. You turned to your left to find the empty bed. You furrowed your eyebrows thinking where Jungkook is? You got up and went towards the bathroom to find it empty. You made your way downstairs but suddenly a mouth watering smell made its way towards your nose. You headed towards the kitchen finding Jungkook looking adorable in his messy hairs and baggy clothes, cooking pancakes for breakfast. You smiled at his cute yet responsible state. Your coming footsteps caught his attention and he turned around to look at you with his big doe eyes.

"Good morning honey~ " he cooed in your ears and gave you a sweet morning kiss. "Morning kook!! " "Are you better now kitten?? " you nodded and he hugged you. "Okay come on, now take a relaxing shower, breakfast is almost done. " "Okay.. " You smiled at him, kissed his cheek then went upstairs to freshen up.

After taking a shower, you changed into a baby pink sweater with white pants. You dried your hair and after freshening up completely, you made your way towards the kitchen and sat down on the dining table. The breakfast was already set up, so you began to choke in the food.

"Mmm.. Its amazing kook. Seriously your cooking made my day. " He beemed at your beautiful comment and began to eat his food too. By the time, you both were watching a movie and enjoying your selves a little, suddenly Jungkook's phone rang. He picked up the call and listened to the person. "Oh.. Yeah okay, wait I will come..... Okay take care of this.. I'm coming, bye. " he sighed. You looked at him with concerned eyes, "koo, what happened? " "Huhh.. I'm sorry baby but I have to go now. An urgent meeting came. They have come from Japan for a research project and want it to discuss with me. " Your face dropped at the thought of his sudden departure. He noticed it and gave your pouty lips a passionate kiss. "Don't worry baby, I will be back soon and we can enjoy our time then, okay? " "Okay, I will wait for you. "

He smiled and made his way towards the bedroom to get ready for his meeting. After getting ready, he came downstairs, put on his shoes and grabbed his car keys. He opened the front door, then turned around again to kiss you. You both broke the kiss and connected your foreheads with each other while smiling at each other softly. You tip toed to kiss him again but this time with a little passion. He broke the kiss, bid you goodbye and went towards his car and drove to the meeting place. And then you were left in the huge house, alone!!

You were done cleaning the house and doing other chores, and now you were sitting on the couch watching the T.V. You were so immersed in the k-drama that suddenly the telephone rang through the whole living room making you flinch. You turned down the volume, stood up and made your way towards the telephone. You picked it up, held it near your ear and spoke, "Hello?" There was no one speaking through the phone. "Helloo?... "

Suddenly the call got cut and you shrugged it of thinking that it may be a wrong number. You again sat on the couch and began to watch your drama.

Again after sometine, the telephone rang making you groan. You turned off the T.V and picked up the phone. "Hello??" you angrily spoke but stopped after. There were some weird shuffling sounds along with someone speaking but you couldn't understand it. "Hello? Who are you? Whom have you called?" You again spoke up. But really couldn't understand what the person was saying. Slowly the voice became a little understandable making you froze at your spot.

"Leave the house,leave the house, leave the house" "wh-what" your voice came like a whisper. "leave the house, leave tHE HOUSE, LEAVE THE HOUSE NOWWWWW" "AHHHH...." You dropped the receiver on the floor, and began shaking. You plugged out the wire of the telephone with your shaking hands and put the switch plug on the table. You stumbled towards the couch, immediately sat down and began to take deep breaths to calm yourself down a little. You kept telling yourself in between your breaths, "its nothing... its nothing.... Y/n,.. You're hallucinating. You're hallucina_" Then again the telephone began to ring but with its main wire UNPLUGGED.

Part 4

You froze at the spot. The telephone continued ringing to the point you couldn't bear it. You stood up, hurried towards the phone, picked it up and began to hit it with the table harshly. Your were crying while hitting it and continued hitting it to the point where it had broken badly. You threw it on the floor. At this point, you were crying badly. You grabbed your hair and ruffled them. The whole scenario made your knees go weak and you fell on your knees to the ground. Your mind wanted to believe that it wasn't true but your heart told you that it's the truth at all.

At this point, you were sure that you aren't hallucinating anymore. Slowly you got yourself together, stood up from your spot and went towards the front door. Your mind wanted peace and you were stressed too much. You decided to take a walk in the neighbor hood. Because nature has peace and it also helped you every time when you got stressed. You walked along the road. It was a lot cold there because of the winter season. The big tall trees were blocking the sun light to reach towards the surface. And this whole scene made your body calm a little.

You were enjoying yourself when a wandering dog came towards you. Its fluffy and silky body got your attention. You kneeled down towards it and began stroking the dog. You saw around yourself to find if its master was nearby. But no one was there. So you decided to head back home along with the dog. You came back home, and opened the front door then went inside. You turned to your back to see the dog standing outside. " Hey buddy, come on get inside. " But he didn't even move. You pulled his neck chain but still he wasn't coming inside.

Suddenly, he began barking while looking inside the house. You were actually standing beside him. You got confused by seeing him barking too much while looking into the living room and not you. Then, he began to move backwards while barking nonstop. His barks got loud from time to time. But at the sudden, he stopped and his eyes got darker. He laid at the doorstep with his head on the floor and closed his eyes. You were super confused at that time. You were looking at the dog but then looked inside to see the floor all dirty.

You got scared because you had cleaned the floor before. But now it had like merged footprints everywhere. You stepped inside the house and saw the footprints scattered in each and every corner of the floor. You moved forward inside the room discovering more merged but odd looking footprints. But then, at the end of the room, the scattered footprints were now unscattered and going towards the hallway. You peeked into the hallway and saw the footprints going inside the basement door and the door was wide open.

You were afraid to go down the basement, so you went towards its door, closed it and then locked it. Then you cleaned the living room floor. You were now sitting on the couch and relaxing your muscles a bit because of cleaning the floor second time in the day. But what made you confuse was that the dog wasn't coming inside. He wasn't even coming towards the doorstep now. You had chained him in the lawn. All the things that had happened today and also your confusing thoughts made you a bit sleepy. Before you could even know, you fell asleep on the couch.

You woke up from your sleep and saw that you were still on the couch. That meant that Jungkook hadn't arrived from the meeting yet. You stood up and went towards the shared bedroom. But when you entered the bedroom, you saw Jungkook laying on the bed with his eyes closed. You furrowed your eyebrows that he had arrived already and didn't wake you up. That made you nervous a lot because whenever you slept on the couch, Jungkook has always lifted you in his arms and laid you on the bed in your shared bedroom.

"Kook, when did you come back? " " When you were sleeping. " he said without even looking at you. You furrowed your eyebrows and asked, " You should have wake me up so I could make you dinner. " " I wasn't hungry at all that's why I didn't wake you up. " he said all of this without opening his eyes and sparing a glance at you. Now this made you confused a lot and you asked him, " Kook are you upset with me? " At this, he opened his eyes and looked at you in the eyes. But what you saw was all dryness and rudeness in his galaxy eyes. " No, why would I ? " he said in a not interested tone. You were sure something's wrong with him. But you shrugged it of and told him that you are going to make yourself dinner.

You went downstairs and made your way to the kitchen. You were cooking food when your phone dinged showing that you have got a message. You opened your phone and read the message only to be frozen at your spot and mind to be numb.

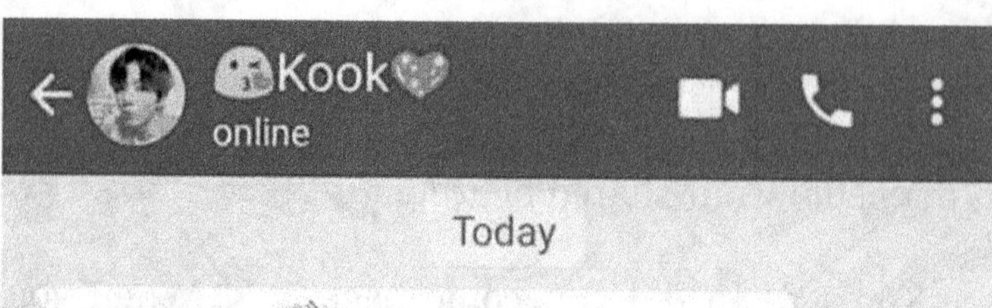
Kook
online
Today
Hey baby ! I'm finally coming back home along with the food . I missed you SOOOO MUCH !!...
08:40
Type a message

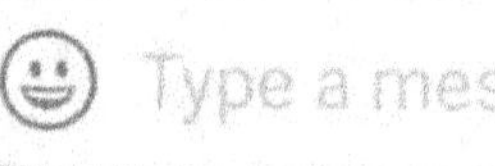

Part 5

Your feet were frozen to the ground yet your mind was fully numb. You thought, he was messing with you. Your heart was beating uncontrollably. It was like your heart wanted you to believe what the actual situation is but your mind was stubborn, yet, YOU were the stubborn creature. You didn't wanted to believe every single thing that had happened before and what is gonna happen next in this DAMN HOUSE.

You thought he was just messing with you but his earlier behavior was seem to be odd.

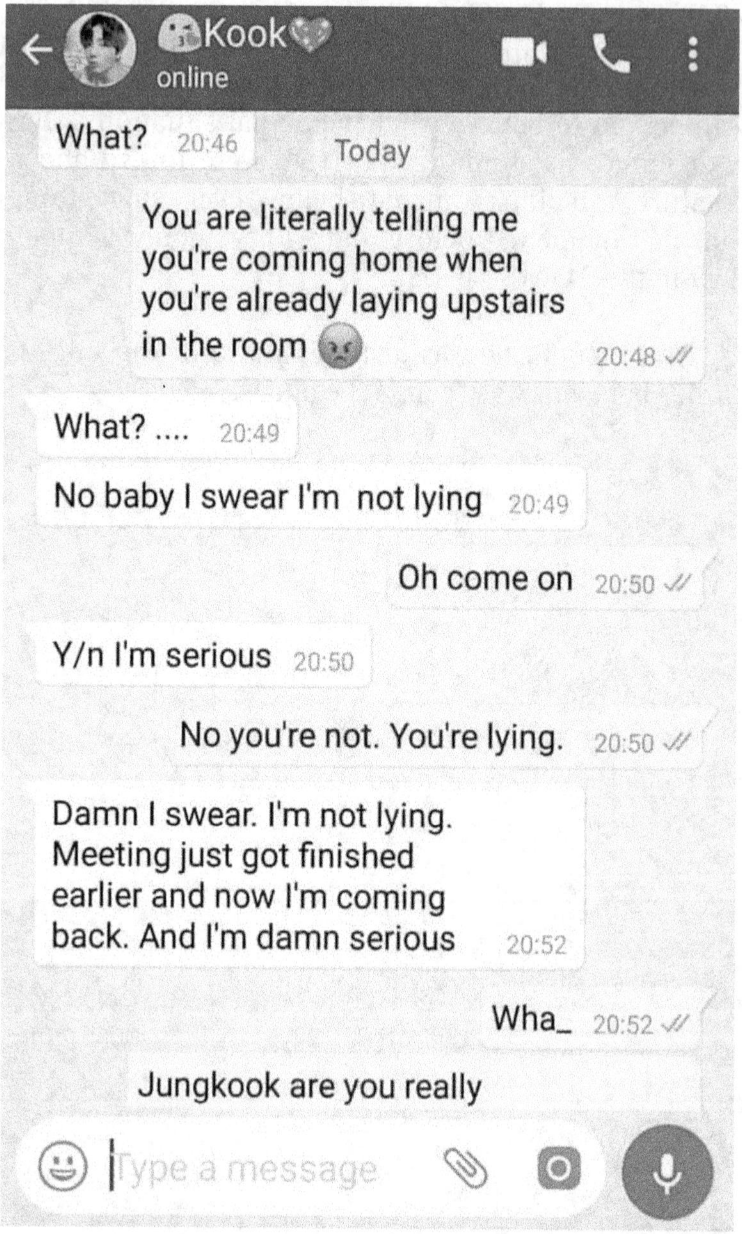

Kook
online

What? 20:46

Today

You are literally telling me
you're coming home when
you're already laying upstairs
in the room   20:48

What? 20:49

No baby I swear I'm not lying 20:49

Oh come on 20:50

Y/n I'm serious 20:50

No you're not. You're lying. 20:50

Damn I swear. I'm not lying.
Meeting just got finished
earlier and now I'm coming
back. And I'm damn serious 20:52

Wha_ 20:52

Jungkook are you really

Type a message

Today

Wha_ 20:52

Jungkook are you really telling me the truth? 20:53

Of course baby why would I lie to you. 20:53

Then who's the person laying on our bed 20:53

?? 20:54

What do you mean by person laying on the bed 20:54

Don't joke around.. 20:54

NO JUNGKOOK I'M NOT JOKING 20:54

LITERALLY THERE IS A DAMN PERSON LAYING ON THE BED AND I THOUGHT IT WAS YOUUUU 20:55

 Type a message   

WAS YOUUI Today   20:55 ✓✓

No y/n I didn't even arrived
yet.   20:56

JUNGKOOK PLEASE PLEASE
TELL ME YOU ARE HOME   20:57 ✓✓

PLEASE PLEASE   20:57 ✓✓

Baby you may have got it
wrong   20:58

Calm down 20:58

I'm just near the home 20:59

JUNGKOOK YOU'RE
LITERALLY TELLING ME TO
CALM THE FUCK DOWN   20:59 ✓✓

PLEASE GET HERE NOW 21:00 ✓✓

I'M SO SCARED 21:00 ✓✓

Okay don't freak out I'm just

 Type a message   

LITERALLY TELLING ME TO
CALM THE Today DOWN   20:59 ✓✓

PLEASE GET HERE NOW   21:00 ✓✓

I'M SO SCARED   21:00 ✓✓

Okay don't freak out I'm just
near btw   21:00

 please just calm down   21:01

YAHHH y/n reply me   21:02

Don't scare me like that   21:02

Come on baby........   21:02

Y/N, PLEASE DON'T SCARE
THE SHIT OUT OF ME   21:03

HELLOO   21:03

DAMNIT   21:03

.... 21:05

Baby?   21:06

Type a message

You were freaking out while messaging him. You still thought of him pranking with you. You mean like DAMN HE IS A GREAT PRANKSTER. So who wouldn't think of it as a prank. When you sent him the last message, someone suddenly back hugged you. Your phone fall from your hands to the ground. The person's breath was hitting your neck and you were like fixed to your spot.

" Hey baby, missed me? " The person's voice was hoarse and it sent shivers down your spine. Your breath was hitched and your voice was stuck down your throat. You whole body began to shiver still in the person's embrace. " j-j-jungkook, huh i-is tha-t y-you huh? " you asked but no one spoke. Now the person removed his arms from your body. But the breath hitting on your neck only got fast. You slowly turned around but when you completely turned back, no one was standing there. But you still felt like someone is breathing near your face. You still felt like someone is watching you but you couldn't see it.

You were still at your spot but then suddenly, all the lights turned off themselves and the whole house became dark. You screamed at the top of your lungs. Your hands searched for your phone but it was nowhere to be found. You moved to the outside with the help of your hands, feeling the walls and the kitchen door. When you got in the living room, you heard some door creaking noise. It was like coming from the hallway. Your eyes couldn't see anything but your heart could sense someone's presence in your house. You heard someone's steps as if the person was coming your way. By the time, your cheeks were flooded with uncontrollable tears flowing down your cheeks, dropping to the floor. You again took a step forward but as if someone pushed you and you fell down on the floor with a large thud.

"W-huh-WHO'S THERE?" Your voice was submerged with your tears. Now you felt like the footsteps were all the way near you, coming right towards you. It felt like a presence near you, standing right behind you ready to do what ever it want, with you. You shut your eyes close tightly. But then, you didn't feel anything, as if your heart was telling you that you were alone in the living room. You slowly opened your eyes only to see the lights turned on now and you were close to the coffee table. You turned your head to your back but there was no one. You saw around every where but no one seemed to be there in the living room.

But as if your sixth sense was working and telling you that you were still not alone. Your heart was beating at a very fast rate and you were breathing very hard. Slowly, you moved your head upwards only to be your eyes widen. There you saw a dark, black, weird and scary looking creature hanging with its hands and legs on the ceiling and it was piercing with its bloodshot eyes right through your soul. Suddenly that creepy creature fell right over you and you shut your eyes close. You began to scream, laying there on the floor. You felt like someone was scratching your arms and trying to scratch your face with its long nails.

By the time, Jungkook had reached the home. He parked his car in the driveway in a hurry and opened the car door, closed it and ran towards the front door. When he reached there, he heard your uncontrollable screams and began to bang on the door.

"Y/N, Y/N OPEN THE DOOR. BABY OPEN THE DAMN DOOR... " But you weren't stopping screaming and that made him terrified. So then he began to hit the door with his shoulder because he didn't have the keys. Suddenly the door got open and he barged in. He saw you laying, rolling on the floor, hands covering your face and you were screaming nonstop.

He rushed towards you, kneeled down and put his arms around you. But you pushed him thinking that he was not Jungkook. "NOOOOOOO GET AWAY FROM MEE GET AWAY,... STOPPPPPP.. " "Y/N ITS ME, LOOK AT ME, Y/N ITS ME DON'T BE AFRAID. YOU'RE SAFE Y/N.... ITS ME I'm here baby calm down I'm here.. " You stopped pushing him and wrapped your arms around his waist tightly to not let him go.

He put your head on his lap and began to stroke your hair to calm you down, knowing that it will help you to calm down. You were still crying a lot but felt safe in Jungkook's embrace. He began to speak soothing words into your ears, lifted you up a little and hugged you tightly. After sometime, you calmed down a little. You moved your head a little only to see in his sparkling eyes which had held a lot of worry for you at that moment.

He kissed your forehead and left a few light pecks here and there. You were still sniffing a lot. " Kook I'm scared. " you whispered in his chest. " I'm scared a lot. Please I don't want to stay here. I can feel like there is someone in this house. No I don't feel, its true kook. There is someone in this house other than us. I can feel its eyes on me. Jungkook I can feel its presence, please please I don't want to live alone, anymore. "

" Baby I'm sure you must took it wrong, there's no one. There's no one in this house EXCEPT US.

You must be hallucina_" " NO JUNGKOOK NOOOOO. I'M NOT HALLUCINATING ANYMORE. I'M SURE,

I'M FULLY SURE. I'M NOT LYING. THERE IS SOMEONE IN THIS HOUSE. FIRST I FELT ITS PRESENCE IN THE BASEMENT YET NOW... I FEEL IT IN THE WHOLE HOUSE. IT IS LIKE SICKNESS EVERYWHERE IN THIS DAMN HOUSE. EVERY NIGHT WHEN I GO TO KITCHEN JUST TO DRINK WATER, I FEEL SOMEONE'S EYES ON ME JUNKOOK, PIERCING RIGHT THROUGH MY SOUL. ITS INTENSE STARE, I CAN FEEL EVERYTHING JUNGOOK. I'M NOT HALLUCINATING. PLEASE BELIEVE ME PLEASE HUHHH please... " you were now sobbing hard and Jungkook was staring at you without blinking his eyes. But then he sighed and spoke up something, which you were afraid to hear. Afraid that he will think that about you.
" I, 'sigh', I think we should see a psychiatrist for you. "

Part 7

"W-What...... Jungkook.... y-you are saying that I-I'm a p-psycho? " he sighed. "Look y/n.. that's not what I mean_" "then WHAT.. Huh what do you mean? " " Y/N listen, you are already tired. Let's sleep. Look tomorrow I will ask the property dealer about all of this, okay? Come on (he cupped your cheeks) let's sleep. Hmm? " You looked into his sparkling eyes with your teary ones. Your lips were trembling with fear yet you still nodded. He smiled a little to encourage you and pecked your trembling lips. He then guided your shaking figure to bedroom. He did his night routine first then you. After brushing your teeth, you stared at yourself in the bath mirror. You were still thinking about the "psychiatrist" thing. You were afraid that he will not believe you and will think that you are a psychopath.

This brought tears in your eyes again but you decided not to lose hope and splashed water on your face. You got out of the bathroom and saw your husband already laying on bed waiting for you. He forwarded his hand and you placed your tiny hand on his. You laid onto the bed next to him. He brought you closer to his body and cuddled with you. You were already tired from all the happenings so you both immediately fell asleep.

Bright sunlight peeking through the glass wall made you squint your eyes a little. You opened your eyes but what you got to see first was your husband's cute face. His chubby cheeks were pressed into the pillow and lips slightly parted. His arms were wrapped around your waist, safely and tightly. This brought a bright smile to your face which gave you some mental relief from all the tension. You brought your hands to his cheek and caressed it lightly. This brought a tingling sensation to his body which woke him up. He opened his eyes to see your beautiful face. He smiled at you and placed his hand above yours and brought it to his lips to kiss your palm gently. "Good morning baby" "Good morning hun" "How was your sleep? " "Good " Your response gave him a happy sensation and he smiled brightly towards you and then kissed your lips. "Come on , take a relaxing shower. I will make breakfast today ok. " You nodded your head like a child and then got off the bed.

You headed to the bathroom to take a shower. Jungkook then headed downstairs into the kitchen to make pancakes. After a relaxing shower, you wore your clothes, got out of the bathroom, dried your hair and then headed downstairs. You walked into the kitchen to see breakfast already served on the table. When Jungkook saw you coming, he smiled and wrapped his arms around you. He kissed your lips and said, "Come on let's eat. I'm very hungry. " You both ate breakfast and then went into the living room.

You both sat on the couch and Jungkook brought you to his embrace. You put your head on his chest and began to listen his calming heartbeat. "I will call the property dealer to tell him to meet us okay. Maybe he can tell us about those happenings. " You nodded. He then kissed your head. " Don't worry every thing will be fine. " Later, he called the property dealer to ask him to meet them and the property dealer informed him to meet at 2pm.

You both were cuddling on the couch. The doorbell rang indicating that the property dealer has arrived. Jungkook got up and went to open the door. The property dealer Mr. Wang came in and greeted you both. Jungkook led him towards the couch. Later you served him with the tea. After some other talkings, Jungkook decided to ask the question for which he had called him. " Um... Mr. Wang, I actually invited you here because we both wanted to ask you about something. So maybe you could tell us about this. " "Of course. What is it? " Jungkook took a deep breath before explaining,

"So there are some weird things happening since the day we came into this house. These things happen every day and my wife has felt them many times. " Mr. Wang tensed a bit after hearing this and asked, "What things Miss Y/n?Can you tell me?" You cleared your throat and then started off.

"Okay... I have felt like there is someone in this house other than us. I can feel its presence here but its not like calming. Its like.. some kind of devil ones. I feel a lot of sickness in this house and about that presence, I think, it doesn't want us to live here. Wherever I go, it feels like it is following me and if I would turn around, it will be right behind me. But when I turn, there's no one. At nights, I feel someone's eyes on me like it is piercing through my soul and will tear me apart. " You stopped and made an eye contact with Mr. Wang, then said, " I think... there is a BAD SOUL in this house who will kill me and my husband sooner or later. "

Mr. Wang's eyes widened and sweat began to form on his forehead. Jungkook sensed some kind of fear in his eyes and asked, " Mr. Wang, are you okay? Please tell us if there's something wrong in this house? " " no no this can't be. This can't be happening. THIS IS IMPOSSIBLE. THAT SOUL WAS LOCKED IN THE BASEMEN_wait.. "

Your eyes suddenly widened. Your heart began to race by hearing basement's name. Mr. Wang noticed your tensed expression and asked you. " Miss y/n, are you involved in this? " His eyes showed nothing but terror, like he is afraid that something bad will happen.

" I-I was just wandering around the house but I heard a weird noise coming from a room. I thought I hadn't seen this room so I went inside. But its door was already opened a little, I swear I didn't open it. " " OMG... Its not going to be good. " " What do you mean by not good? Mr. Wang, please tell us. " Jungkook asked with desperateness. Mr. Wang took a deep breath before speaking, " Okay, there was a bad soul locked in the basement and its door was completely locked but I think that somehow, it has opened. And now... That soul is free from being locked. And now, it is haunting you guys." There was a long and frightful pause until you spoke. "But.. Mr. Wang, we still can leave this house. I mean if we leave then it will stop haunting us right?

" You were afraid of the answer by seeing Mr. Wang's dropped expression. " I'm sorry to say this Mrs. Jeon but... If you leave this house, then wherever you both go... That soul will FOLLOW YOU.

Part 8

You were in your shared bedroom. Jungkook was in bathroom taking a shower while you were sitting on your bed fiddling with your fingers. Your mind was lost at that moment and your thoughts were still focused on those talkings. Mr. Wang's words were revolving again and again around your head making you unconscious about your surroundings. Jungkook came out of the bathroom wearing comfy clothes and a towel in his hands, drying his hair. He saw you with your lost expression, he knew you were still thinking about Mr. Wang's words which he said before. He sighed, put the towel on a chair and made his way towards you. Jungkook sat beside you yet you still didn't notice his presence beside you. He was looking at his fingers when he said your name softly but you were lost so much that you didn't give him a response. He moved his eyes towards you and kept his hand above yours. " Y/n? " You suddenly flinched at his remark and looked in his eyes. You could see the tension, the worries he was holding in his eyes at that time.

You both spoke nothing, just stared into each other's eyes until you broke the contact and stared at your lap again. " Do you think what Mr. Wang said is true? " You asked him softly without looking into his eyes. " You think that soul will follow us every where? " You were still staring down when you heard him sighing softly. He took a deep breath then spoke softly, " You know.. Sometimes... Situations would seem understandable, the happenings around us seem clear but... Our hearts don't want to believe them. We DO want to believe the reality but our hearts don't. And that's what happening with us. We do want to believe this but our hearts, our minds aren't convinced much about all of this. BUT there is something that I know for sure. And that is,...

Whatever happens around us or with us, I will ALWAYS be with you... No matter what. I don't care about whatever is going to happen but what I care about the most is.... Not to leave this hand, not to leave your side, Till. Death. Do. Us. Apart. I love you and that's what matters the most. "

He was staring the whole time in your eyes and you could see the sincerity in his words as well as in his sparkling, galaxy holding eyes. At the end, you smiled softly at him and said, " I love you too kook. I love you so SOO much. You don't have any idea how much you matter to me. How much you worth to my heart, to myself. I'm so lucky to have you. Thank you for everything kook... I love you more. " "... And I love you the most " You both stared into each other's eyes while smiling brightly at each other before leaning in and softly connecting your lips with each other in a life holding kiss. After the lovely session, you both said ' GOODNIGHT ' to each other and laid down on the bed. He held you close to his body and cuddled with you. Lastly, he kissed your forehead then you both slept in each others embrace.

You both were sleeping soundly in each other's embrace. Suddenly there was a knock at the front door of the house but the sound was too low to be heard. But then, the knocking got loud by the time which woke Jungkook up. He thought that he may got it wrong so he decided to sleep but then again, he heard loud knocks at the door. He got up from the bed and saw the time. He was very much confused because he didn't expect any visitor at that time. He went downstairs and headed to the door. " Who's there?... " Jungkook asked but no one answered. He watched through the peep whole but didn't see anyone outside. He opened the door, looked around but again, there was nobody to be found. He got confused but then got inside and locked the door.

He was on his way towards the bedroom but then again heard the knocking at the door. He flinched and jolted in his steps. He was confused a lot and thought that maybe somebody was messing around. So he aggressively made his way towards the door and bursted it open. But then again, he was met with no one. He got outside the house and decided to look around. He looked through every corner but didn't see anybody. Again, he made his way inside of the house and locked the door. But when he turned around and made a step forward, he stepped on something. He looked down and saw the weird doll again under his foot. He bent down and picked it up. He was confused at first but then his eyes widened at the remembrance. He remembered putting that doll on the piano table. He was shockingly looking at that odd stuffed doll but then, he heard a creak sound. He got goosebumps at the sudden sound. He didn't look up at first but then slowly moved his eyes at his front and saw you standing in front of him at the end of the stairs. You had scratches on your arms and neck. You hair were a lot messy, clothes dirty and your eyes were dark piercing right through his eyes. You had a very cliche smirk on your face. His eyes widened at your state and his words were like stuck in his throat. He was shocked to see you in that wrecked state. " y-y/n.... What h-happened to you-" He was stuttering due to utter shock. But then you began to laugh hysterically at his question. "What?.. Shocked to see me.. In this state, right? But don't worry.... I will make your state more wrecked..... And make you both suffer.... A lot (whispered).

Just wait and watch " Right when you finished talking, a flower vase came flying through the air and crashed on jungkook's head resulting into pieces. But the harsh contact made Jungkook's knees gone week and he fell on the ground with blood coming out of his forehead and KNOCKED OUT.

Part 9

Alone in the bed, you felt a little cold not being in your husband's arms. You opened your eyes a little to see Jungkook's spot empty. You moved to see the time but a little frown made on your face by seeing the time being 3 am. You sat on your bed to see the bathroom empty and its light off. ' Maybe he is in the kitchen. ' you said to your self. You wore your shoes and walked to the door. You opened the room door and walked out of the room. You went downstairs but stopped abruptly in your steps. Your face became pale and eyes widened at the sight in front of you. Jungkook was there, laying unconscious on the floor with blood all around his head and on the floor. " JUNGKOOKKK....." You speedily walked down the stairs and ran towards him. "OMG JUNGKOOK.... WHAT HAPPENED... " You put his head on your lap and began to check his pulse. It was low to the minimum. You didn't know when your tears began to stream down on your cheeks. You looked around and saw many broken pieces of the flower vase on the floor and thought that maybe his head hit hard on that vase. You carefully laid Jungkook's head on the floor and sprinted towards your room to get your phone. You called the ambulance and they quickly made their way to your home.

"Kook....Baby stay there please....stay with me......." You were sobbing hard while hugging Jungkook's body which was getting weaker minute by minute.

After 10 minutes, you heard sirens meaning that the ambulance has arrived. You quickly walked to door and opened it for the ambulance attenders (I don't know what we call them in specific). They brought a stretcher in and laid Jungkook on it and quickly brought him inside the ambulance. " Miss are you coming too? " " yes " They let you in and the ambulance made its way

34

to the hospital. After reaching there, the nurses quickly brought him to the operation theater. You were told to stay outside so you went to a chair and sat down lazily. You were staring blankly at your feet yet your mind was full of concern for Jungkook. You were praying for him to stay safe and healthy. Your tears were mindlessly falling on your cheeks yet your expression still remained blank.

You were still sitting at the same spot for two hours. You didn't move an inch from there but your mind was stuffed with concern and worry. After sometime, the door to the operation theater opened and they brought Jungkook's body outside. You immediately stood up and went towards him. His head was bandaged but he was still unconscious. You brought your hands to caress his cheeks. But some seconds later, they dragged the stretcher away from you to shift him in a room. " Doctor.. Please tell me how's he? " " The surgery went successful and the patient is now out of danger. (you sighed in relief) But...there is one more thing. " Your heart was beating very fast at the moment yet you still gathered the courage to ask the question. " What is it?... " " The impact on patient's head was very hard due to which he has lost quite amount of blood. His brain is weak at the moment and we... *sigh*.. I'm sorry but we can't say when he will be able to wake up!! " The news was like someone stabbed right in your heart and your heart dropped by hearing it. " Just hope he wake up soon! " and with that, the doctor walked away. You immediately broke down at the instant, you were praying hard for him to wake up because you couldn't see the love of your life, the king and only owner of your heart in that condition.

You asked a nurse if you could stay beside him and she said yes. You jogged towards his room and after taking a deep breath to not lose hope, you opened the door and went inside. There he was, laying on the hospital bed looking weak as hell with tubes surrounding his body. There was an oxygen mask on his face to help him breath in that weak state and also a glucose drip attached to his right hand to provide some energy to his weak and pale body. You dragged your feet towards his bed and stood beside him. His heart beat showing on a monitor was running at a slow rate. You began to caress his left cheek lightly yet softly. If someone had told you a few hours ago that he will be in this state after sometime then you wouldn't have believe him but now he was in his weakest state. You couldn't help but shed a few tears along with a soft sob remembering how his big doe and galaxy eyes used to stare right into yours along with a bright bunny smile on his face. But now he was still. His face was blank, his eyes were closed. There wasn't any kind of expression on his face. It was like his life was slowly advancing towards the death. "NO!.... Nothing will happen to you kook. I won't let you die....You promised to me that you would stay with me forever and now... You HAVE to fulfill that promise baby. You have to keep fighting for me, for yourself. For us. You have to keep fighting for our relationship kook. I can't lose you....I can't!! " That's it. You determined to not break down in front of him but still couldn't help with yourself. You could accept anything. You could accept poverty, you could accept hate, you could accept yourself to die but you couldn't accept to live without him. Him, he was him,

Who made your heart flutter at the first sight. Who brought not only butterflies but a whole zoo inside your stomach. Who made you accept the love at first sight concept. Who, with his tiny little cute tasks, made your heart warm. Who with his soft yet gentle touch brought a crimson blush on your cheeks. Who with his love confession made your heart skip a beat. Who with his doe eyes and a cute pout made you love him even more. And who with his ethereal vow gave you hope, a strong hope which confirmed the thought that he was the one. The one who is called as your soulmate. The one with whom, you will spend the rest of your life and were determined to spend the rest of your life with. THAT'S HIM. Whom you can't lose at any given cost. He was the one for you whom you loved with your whole heart and whom you will love till your last breath. Because he was your source of breathing and if there's no him, then there would be no you. And with that thought, you decided only to do one thing which was pray. You decided that this was the only way which could make him live to the fullest. Which could keep him SAFE AND ALIVE!

Part 10

Some muffled voices could be heard yet still you kept your eyes closed. But then you felt a pat on your shoulder. " Mam... Please wake up". You abruptly woke up from your nap. Vision was blur but after sometime you analyzed your surroundings. You were sitting on the side of your husband's bed. He was still unconscious but his face color changed a bit to normal. It wasn't pale now. " Mam can you please go outside, I have to check the patient's condition " You nodded at her request and stood up from your seat. You lightly kissed Jungkook's cheek and headed outside the room.

Thoughts were overflowing your mind. How did this happened? Why didn't you hear anything? Your mind was a stuffed with all the tensions that you couldn't summarize anything. You were pacing back and forth in the hallway. Crowds of people were everywhere and the atmosphere in there wasn't helping. So you went outside.

There was garden at the back of the hospital so you went there and sat on a bench. The breeze was better there than inside. You moved your eyes towards the sky and put your head on the head of bench. The sky was covered with loads of clouds yet it was still bright. But it would have been better if Jungkook was there with you. Even the thought brought tears in your eyes and you shed a few of them. How beautiful and peaceful your life was before you shifted in this house.

No one, literally NO ONE warned you or told you anything about that soul which had now made your life a living hell. It was like you were facing the punishments of your wrong doings. Yet still you wondered if you did anything much worse to deserve a punishment like that. You were in your own world of thoughts that you flinched when your phone rang. You brought it out of your pocket and saw an unknown number. This unknown number made you remember the phone calls of that unknown person on the telephone.

The thoughts of that voice brought chills in your spine. You didn't want to face any incident like that so you didn't pick up the call. Your phone stopped ringing but after sometime it rang again. It was that unknown number again. You looked at your surroundings and saw some people which gave you a bit confidence to face this unknown call.

You gathered a little courage and then swiped to pick up the call. You brought the phone to your right ear and waited for someone to speak from the other side. When no one spoke you cleared your throat and spoke up. " h-hello? " your voice came out hoarse and you were a bit terrified to listen to the response from the person.

"Is this Mrs. Jeon? " With that you heaved a sigh and spoke further. " Yes, I am. Who are you? " " Oh its me, Mr. Wang. " " Oh. Its you. Sorry I was a bit busy so.. couldn't pick up the call. " " No its totally ok. Actually I wanted to talk to Mr. Jeon about something but he isn't picking my calls. So I wanted to ask if you could tell me where he is. " " jungkook?.... He won't be able to pick your calls. " " What? But why is that? Is he busy? "

Your lips quivered, you were near to bring out a sob but still controlled yourself. " H-he is in hospital. " " WHAT? But- how? " " I found him injured in the living room at night and brought him here. " your tears were now flowing like a waterfall, your whole body was shaking due to emotions you had controlled to bring out. " In which hospital are you, tell me. I will come " " He is in the City Hospital (a hospital of my own :P) " " Ok don't worry Ms. Y/n. I will be there in a while. " with that you cut off the call and brought out a sob cause now you couldn't hold your emotions inside your weak heart.

He was sitting with his elbows on his knees and head down after I narrated the whole incident of jungkook's accident. There was silence but my sniffing nose was covering up the awkward silence between us. I was in my own world of sadness and he was in his own world of thoughts. "I'm really sorry this all happened to you and Mr. Jeon. Literally I'm so sorry. " "You really SHOULD! " My voice came out harsh but hoarse due to crying a lot. "If it wasn't for you then he wouldn't have been here. In fact, we wouldn't even be in all this misery JUST if it wasn't for YOU! You are the cause of all of this and you really should be sorry of your mistakes Mr. Wang! "

He sighed after listening to my bursted anger. I know he's older than me, even the age of my father but what he did was unacceptable. He could have opened up his mouth . He could really have told us all of that but no, he didn't. Being a property dealer of that big house may have made him greedy or God knows what when we offered to live in the house which was neglected by every other customer. If greed made him keep his mouth shut, then being sorry was the least he could do.

"I'm ready Mrs. Jeon.. " Turning to me and speaking this out made me confused. What's even that thing for which he's ready for. "I'm ready to take the blame Mrs. Jeon... I'm ready to repent for all my sins. I'm ready to make all your miseries disappear.... And I'm also ready to save Mr. Jeon! " "s-save him? What do you mean? " His eyes were shinning bright. There was this determinism in them that made me believe he really is gonna be a man of his words. "You really think Mr. Jeon is in Coma? " "What are you trying to say Mr. Wang? Of course he is in Coma. He is in his worst state and the doctors can't even comprehend exactly when is he going to wake up! " He brought out a sigh. Like he wasn't gonna believe me. His expressions showed it all. He had something in his own mind which I could bet was totally different from my thoughts, totally opposite to my perspectives. "He is not... He isn't in Coma Ms. Y/n. You might be thinking that him not waking up is because he is in Coma and of course doctors will conclude on this. But I know, he is not.... He is asleep Ms Y/n. His body is in this world but his soul is not. Spiritually his soul is in another world. A world where we humans can't go unless we sleep or die. Everytime when a person dies, we think he/she is now vanished. The chapter is totally closed but its not that. We still can meet the soul cause you already know that when a soul leaves the body, then it stops functioning and becomes static. We can still communicate to the soul. But not every time the communication goes correct. If it goes the wrong way then we might make our lives a living hell. That's how Sophia became a bad soul. " "wait-who's Sophia? " "... The soul in your house. Making your lives hell and haunting you in your sleeps. She died at a very young age. 18 I guess. But her parents couldn't accept her death cause she was a lot dear to them. The dearest among all their children. So then, they met a priest and asked him to let them communicate to her soul. And when they did, they asked her soul to come and live in their house again cause her presence was enough for them. But... what that priest didn't know was that in the process of a dead soul coming back to the life, many other souls find this out as well. And they try to come as well but the problem is that only One soul can come back in a body. And they only had Sophia's body. So instead of Sophia's soul...there came another soul, the Dangerous one, a Devil. Cause bad souls are more powerful than normal ones and that's how it came in her body and used her body to do every bad work..... It killed Sophia's family. Her siblings, her parents even her aunt living with them at that time. It killed everyone. And all those too who came to live in that house after them..... And now its after you guys. It was locked by a priest in the basement but I dont know how it got out of there and is now trying to do the same with you and your husband which it did with others. Its trying to kill you guys. " "But.... but i read somewhere that dead souls find a body to re-live either in a good way or bad way, its like their only left aim after death. And you telling me all of this, it clearly says that this soul already has Sophia's body so why? Why is it after others now? " "Ms. Y/n you might know that the body without soul remains good in condition for only a specific time. After that it starts decomposing. And in all this time, of course how could that soul rely only on Sophia's body. It needed more bodies with the time being. So till now it has used every body it killed in that house. Now the body, it's using, is getting expired day by day. And its in great need of another body. And now its trying to use Mr. Jeon's body. He is in this condition because of that soul and if we wont do anything urgently .....then I'm sorry but we might lost Mr. Jeon to it! " tick, tick, tick....

Part 11

The ticking of the pendulum clock was adding more awkwardness to the air. Silence was eating you inside. The walls of the oddly looking room were being like a stuffed cage to you. And it didn't do anything but made you nervous, more and more. You were scared. For your life, for your soul, for the one who was more than a soulmate to you. If there was any other word holding more importance than the word "soulmate" itself, still that would be less to explain how much worth Jungkook held in your own heart, in your life. And at this moment, nothing was more dear to you than the health of your dear husband.

The sound of a door opening made you come out of your own world of thoughts. Your eyes moved instinctively to look at there where the sound was coming from. Eyes narrowed, the pupils of your eyes dilated to the darkness of the portion outside that door from where an old lady was coming inside.

She was odd, very strange to you. Her attire, her personality, her aura gave you weird vibes. Your sixth sense was telling you she's just....weird. Of course why not, as she was a paranormal investigator. Strange aura would obviously be in her personality. Coming near the table and sitting in front of you and Mr. Wang, she finally looked up at you, letting her eyes observe you fully. Her eyes looked as if they were trying to study you without acquiring anything, without asking anything, without you explaining anything. She was just.....eye studying you, judging you by your presence, by your acts, how you were concentrated on her actions, how your eyes tried to understand her back, but how nervous you actually were by her doing this, she observed this all. As if on the instinct, she picked the main point and concluded to finally ask or more like tell, you were amazed by her spoken statement.

"She is dangerous! " Your eyes moved to Mr. Wang. Like you, he was fazed as well, from the decision of you both to go tell her and take help to her actually starting the session without knowing anything did surprised you both. "But.... Mrs Madison-how do you-" "I can feel her... Her presence... Its the most sickening one I have ever felt. Her soul, its very desperate. I can sense the need she is in right now. " Her eyes were moving around the room. Slowly, yet very intensely. As if that soul was really here, following you all the way to this destination. The sound coming from her mouth was hoarse, her voice held deepness, pushing the intensity more and more at the words which were meant to show you how important this situation was.

"Your husband, he's helpless right now. In great need of assistance. He's looking for you to come and help him.... Save him y/n. Save him! " your hands making a heavy contact with the desk, you moved your body forward. Looking deep in her eyes, in tries of showing her how confused and helpless you are right now. "Please tell me.. How can I save him? Please help me, I beg you! " You intertwined your fingers, deeply requesting her to help you and she did knew, you would even beg if its for saving your husband, your jungkook.

"Brian David.... Go to him at the Cape Fear town. Once you tell him, he will help you, without asking for help..... Go before it gets too late. "~~Time skip~~

Driving through the town, you looked outside the window at your right, in case if you would see the church that lady told you to go to. "We are there. There it is! " Moving your eyes to the front left, you saw the church. It wasn't a big church but neither a small one. You both got out of the car and went inside. Walking to the front, there was a minister (in case you don't know. Its a person authorized by the church or organization to look after the church). His back was facing you both. He was standing there, with his hands connected praying at that time. You didn't want to disturb him in between so you both sat at the bench behind you both. "what do you think Mr. Wang, will he be able to help us? " He sighed after you asked. Letting his fingers fiddle he spoke afterwards. "To be honest, I'm sure he will. That lady is quite famous. She has been successful in helping every other person in such cases or if can't then still the persons she advises to seek help from also do great. So if you ask, yes I'm hopeful. And you know right now sitting in a church, I can really feel everything will be fine. Just believe in God..hm? " His lines did eased you a bit and you sighed and smiled at him afterwards.

Do you guys need any help? " Looking upwards you saw that priest. He wasn't old. In fact he was still young, maybe in fourty's. You stood up in respect and decided to ask him about that priest. "Hello father, uh actually we came here looking for the priest Brian David. Can you tell us if he's available at the moment. " "My name is Brian. I'm the priest here. " he politely smiled at you and finally, you thanked God to be able to meet him. "Father David, I can finally say we are happy to meet you. We are in great need of help and this lady, actually she's the one who's in need of help. Please assist her, we will be grateful to you. "

"Sure my child. Tell me what made you come here? " You were still nervous, afraid if he would be able to help you or not. Not like it was some business case and you would ask him to pray for it and he will pray but of course, this case was different but maybe not for him.

And this was what making to still rely on him. "Father...
My husband, he is in the hospital. Doctors said he's in
Coma but our instincts are telling us he's not. And that's
why we went to Miss Madison. She told us to meet you
and also that you will help us. " His expressions were
curious. He understood what you guys were here for.
"Its a paranormal case right. " "Yes father. " "Hm can you
tell me where you are living right now, I would visit there
and analyze the situation. " "I'm from Sanford. " "What?
Sanford?   Can you-can you tell me the address? " "
6330 Windsor, Lake circle! " He was astonished. Like he
knew about this house already. ".. Jesus Christ.. " "Father
what happened? " " it's Sophia's case right? " Your breath
got stuck in the throat. " yes.... h-how do you know? " he
took in great amount of air. "I know about this....

My father, he was the priest to whom Sophia's
parents visited for the communication case...... " He
looked me in the eyes, his eyes were shining bright.
I could say my heart lightened seeing this. "You
came at the right place my child. I know what has
happened with you. Don't worry..... I will help you save
your husband!!! "

Part 12

"David's POV" Stepping inside the house, I unknowingly started feeling a bit sick. It felt like everywhere, wherever I would go in the house, would be sickness. In every corner, in every room. Her sinisterity was spread in all the house and my heart was reacting over it. "Where did you feel her presence first? " " uh huh in the... basement " Making our way towards the hallway, we stopped in front of that door. I took a deep breath and mumbled 'God protect us all amen' before opening the door. It was dark, very dark inside. "I will turn the ligh-" "No! Let it be dark! " Slowly moving downstairs we all three reached down. My beats started getting faster than before showing I'm feeling her hear....that she IS here. I instantly pulled out the crucifix from my pocket and held it in front of me.

The sound started coming to my ears. It was all grumpy, a very disturbing sound, like everything was quivering reacting to the crucifix, as if the earth was shaking, bringing the earthquake in existence but I knew it wasn't like that. It was the shakening sound coming from the stuffs placed in here. Just wherever I got the feel of getting closer and closer to "her", there the sound picked the intensity. And it gradually started increasing......

The frequency increased abruptly, as if the earthquake got intense with the time forwarding. Like I was merely twenty steps far than her.... And I did covered that distance as well. Cause the intense sound crossed the boundaries, making all our ears pain with it. I could hear y/n whimpering and I could feel the shaking figure of Wang behind me. "So this is where you are! " And a very strong wave of air shattered us to our depth, shaking our whole figures at the spots, and then, it was quite. All silent, no sound, no shaking of earth, no feelings of that presence. Like it vanished from there... teleported to somewhere, far from there, to not be close to us, to me.....at least not to the crucifix. And I wasn't a fool either.

"In the name of God who is most merciful and kind, giving me a purpose of serving the humanity and fulfilling the rightful responsibilities, I hereby, have come here to fulfill another responsibility, to help these children, to make their lives peaceful and worth living, to provide them the deserving prosperity, to remove the troubles from their lives, help them solve their problems and to BREAK the CURSE OF THIS DISGUSTING SOUL!!! " Her screams started spreading across the basement, I knew she was 'still' here, fooling around with us so it could distract us from our aim. But not now!

"Man is destined to die once, and after that to face judgment! You are already dead. You don't exist in this world, your physical presence has completed its journey from birth to death. And NOW, I Pray to Jesus to GET THE CURSE OF YOUR BAD SOUL BROKEN!!"

"Author's POV" Everything started shattering. The glassy things broke and their pieces spreaded on the floor. It was hell of the moment, so drastic that you would eventually die panicking in this situation.

The wooden wall beneath the stairs as well started making creaky noises. "Oh my God, Father what is happening? Please DO SOMETHING! " You were already shaking to the death. "WANG TAKE HER OUT OF HERE. ITS NOT SAFE FOR HER TO BE HERE... GO! " "y-y-es com'on y/n. LET'S GET OUT OF HERE COM'ON! " You both ran to the stairs but before you could step on them, a strong push of air made you fell on the other corner of the basement. Your body came in contact with the bricky wall first and then fell to the floor. A painful moan made its way out of your mouth, a sound of bone cracking could also be heard indicating that your left shoulder had fractured. "AHHHHH " You started sobbing due to unbearable pain in the left part of your whole body. "Y/N!!! OMG Y/N ARE YOU OKKK?? " Mr. Wang ran towards your lying figure and bent down by your side. "Y/n! Are you ok? Are you hurt anywhere? " He began to hold you from your shoulders in an attempt to stand you up but another painful moan in between the sobbing made him stop. "STOP PLEASE- don't touch me.... huh I-I think my shoulder is f-fractured. " "my god... Y/n can you move? " "I...don't think so. No wait please.... I will stand up on my own. " Slowly moving your body in a position where your back came in contact with the floor, it was hella painful to even move. You took in a deep yet encouraging breath and with the help of Mr. Wang, you slowly sat on the floor. Your right hand was holding your left shoulder making sure it won't move. Because you knew it was fractured and even a slightest movement will make the pain go worse.

"Are you alright?? Is it paining a lot? " You were sniffing, your face was scrunched up in pain. Your nervous nervous system was indeed reacting to the pain, making your nerves take the feels of pain to your spinal cord so you could feel the intensity of pain so as well your body could react to it. "I.. I'm f-fine...Don't worry " it barely came out as a whisper, this much intense was your pain actually. Suddenly the whole basement brightened up. You slowly moved your head upwards to see the light on. The tears in your eyes were reflecting a lot of light rays making them shine in the light. You wandered your gaze around the whole area. Your whimpering came to a halt along with your eyes, stopping at the wall with a fault in it under the stairs.

"what is that? " listening to your voice, both the men moved their gazes to that wall seeing a big fracture in it. Mr. Wang helped you stand up and finally drinking in the pain, you stood up on your feet and followed father David who was now starting to fist punching a little on the cracks. They eventually broke and fell on the inner side of the wall. David looked everywhere in a hurry to see if he could find anything to break the remaining wall. Finally finding an ax on the top of a cupboard, he picked it and started hitting that wooden wall with it. Cracking noises could be heard. It was breaking and cracking as well to the point that finally the whole wall broke eventually. Disgusting, it was a small, very small word you could say after inhaling a sickening smell from inside. "GOSH what's that smell? "

"Is there any light? " "No I don't think so. " Your voice came out hoarse indicating that you were still in pain. "Wait- I have my mobile. let me just....turn the flash on. " after Mr Wang turned the flashlight on, David moved it towards his front. You all gasped, your breath getting stuck in your throat, your right hand making its way to your lips. You were seeing the horrific sight in front of your eyes. Feeling your breath getting uneven and heart to drop in the deepness of disastrousness. Who wouldn't give such a reaction...after seeing disgusting raw bones and dusty bonal bodies inside the space of that wall!!!

Final

"Jesus Christ!! " To say you all were scared was an understatement. You all were terrified to death. Those bones, how could someone explain their condition in words! Decomposed to the worst, emitting disgusting smell not less than any poisonous gas making you all scrunch your noses. "Are these...dead bodies?? " you spoke out being all terrified. "They aren't even in the condition to be called as dead bodies! " "But- whom skeletons are these? " At that time of misery, no one knew what to even think yet speak was beyond the word 'far'. "Do you think these can be of all the people that died in this house? " David was too out of his mind to even comprehend if what Wang just said was right or wrong. "How are you so sure Mr. Wang? " "What's there to be sure of? Of course these bodies are theirs. Its crystal clear.... Look! (Wang moved closer to some bones and pointed at them) These bones, they are at their worst states which means these can be of Sophia's families as they are much decomposed than these. See, how still good in condition these are. Obviously these can be of the families which died after Sophias! "

"I think Mr. Wang is right here. Or else how these bodies could come here? " David took a deep breath and heaved a sigh after. Trying to use his brain at the moment, he quickly thought of some solution to this situation cause of course he came to pray here for the curse to be broken but now these bones. It was so confusing for him now, knowing that he didn't know he would have to come across the raw bones. "If that's the case... " He moved his head and stared into the space "We have to burn these bones. So that whichever body is currently in use.... will burn to ashes. " David moved and looked in you both's eyes "... And her curse would be broken! "

Doing as said, Father David and Mr. Wang brought all those bones out to the backyard of the house so they could burn them without any difficulty. "Let's end this now. Hurry up give me the matchbox! " Mr. Wang searched in his pockets and eventually brought out a lighter hoping it would work technically. Grasping the lighter from his hands, when the friction wheel on the lighter got turned on by David's thumb pressing onto the button, he immediately brought it to the bones and held it close for them to take the ignition but who was he fooling? Of course its not easy to burn a bone alone with a lighter so trying was only a waste of time. "I don't think these will burn this easily. We should use some petrol or anything? " "We should DEFINITELY use it. (David looked at you in eyes and spoke out) Do you have petrol or any other combustible liquid at house? " Making your mind function at a fast speed, you started thinking if you guys had any combustible hydrocarbon available right now or no. And then, it suddenly clicked. "YES. We have kerosene oil. I kept it in a cabinet of the kitchen upstairs. I'll bring it right away. " Moving inside the house, you ran upstairs rushing towards your forward. Reaching the kitchen which was made for the first floor of that house, you started opening the cabinets in hurry searching for the kerosene oil. After searching inside every cabinet under the shelf, you started looking inside the upper cabinets. But due to the shoulder fracture, you were having very much difficulty while standing on your tip toes in search for the combustion oil using only one hand. Minutes after rummaging through stuffs in different cabinets, you finally found the kerosene. Getting happy that its finally gonna end, a bright smile made its way on your face. "I FOUND ITT!! " Picking the bottle with the kerosene inside it, you hurriedly closed the cabinet and turned around when your breath got stuck . You were flinched badly to death when the door to the kitchen slammed loudly and got closed. The lights inside the kitchen started flicking rapidly when one by one, each light blasted into pieces leaving the kitchen darker than before. This is it, it was gonna happen again, and you being not used to it all got your breath heavier than before. Your legs started shaking hearing some creepy footsteps in the kitchen. You weren't prepared for this, and your fear of darkness didn't help either. Soon your knees met the floor with a loud thud and your hands made their way to your ears, trying to block those disturbing sound waves colliding with your ear drums. Your cheeks were wrenched with tears and your face was scrunched up due to the fear. "stay aw-ay" Your sobs got louder with the footsteps coming closer and closer. "Stay AWAY FROM ME!.... I SAID STAY AWAY! " and it all got clear. No sound was heard. The air was all clear but your heart was still beating faster. Your guts still kept telling you that the sight still wasn't clear.

You opened your eyes seeing dark everywhere but nothing could be heard. The pain in your shoulder got worse but it didn't matter. You had to get out of here and that's what you did. Standing up on your feet, you ran towards the door with all your might but as your hands touched the doorknob, you felt a pull on your ankles and at the instant, your body dropped on the floor. Your front came in a harsh contact with the floor that you felt your abdomen press in pain. You felt yourself being dragged away from the door. "AHHH... LEAVE MEEE!! " having your cries ignored, you were dragged and dragged until you reached in the middle of kitchen near the window to the backyard. Your abdomen was hurting due to the constant dragging and the shoulder pain, let's not even talk about that. You got flipped over your back. You were that much afraid and in pain that you kept your eyes closed. You didn't want to see your death with your bear eyes so you kept them shut as hard as you could.

Feeling nothing above you got you relieved for a moment but you knew that's not the time to get at peace. Anything could happen and that's what happened. "Open your eyes baby... " how could this be.... him? This was him, it was jungkook's voice. At this state, your heart was like, it will burst out at any moment. Slowly opening your eyes, you saw him. His bloody face, black dark eyes and the blood dripping out of his mouth on your face didn't do anything but terrified you to your death. You forgot how to breath. It was like that soul really got jungkook's body and now its you whose gonna end up dead. Hicupping and taking in shaky breaths, your body started shaking. Your level of fear couldn't be explained in words. The smirk on his bloody face made your heart drop to depth. And him coming down closer to your face was what made you burst your screams out. Your face was turned to the side, how could you even see the disastrous sight and that's too on top of you. Tears in your eyes made everything blurry for you to see around you. When the sight got cleared, you saw it..... The Kerosene bottle. Having your breath getting heavier, this was it. The only one and last chance. Having his face in this much depth of your neck that he couldn't see anything, you stretched your arm and held the bottle. "If only me... then we will die together. " With that you threw the bottle with all your might outside the window and felt his teeth sink in your soft skin. "BURN THEM NOWWW!"

Epilogue

Hurrying with her steps, she walked through the neighborhood with a bright smile displayed on her face. She was very happy, too much happy that one couldn't even measure it. Finally her life was at peace, that they got such close people as their neighbors. It was like the God was finally being kind on her. The time when her dearest one got to face some hurdles, no one could tell how much her heart was steady now, beating at the normal rate. Reaching at the doorstep, she knocked instantly not wanting to wait anymore but do everything herself to not let her neighbors do anything. The door opened and that's how her brightest smile mixed up with her beautiful neighbors.

Mom! The person's lips stretched upwards seeing her mother at the doorstep. "You finally came. " " *laughing as well* Y/n... my sweetheart!.... " Embracing her daughter with her warm heart, she hugged her tight. Their happiness was out of the limit, it was very difficult to even comprehend their happiness but not that it wasn't displayed. It was shown clearly how her mother was so happy to have her daughter finally as her neighbor. Only God knows how much she had told her that time to shift close to them but....fate had other plans. "Ah~ finally! You are near me... I missed you SO MUCH. " "Me toooo~" Breaking the hug, your mother stared at you as if you had been far, very far from her. As if she hadn't seen you for years. Her eyes held that welcoming shine in them making your mind get at internal peace, that peace which you were deprived off years ago. Your mother chuckled, rubbing your arms so warmly just like a helpless mother, who was in search of her missing dear child and finally found her piece of heart. "You can stare at me now all you want but first come inside. " You both cracked a laugh at the fact that she could really stare lovingly at her daughter even for hours. This was all she ever longed for. A happiest smile on her daughter's face. Lucky you who got such a beautiful kind hearted mother.

Getting inside the house, she removed her shoes she was wearing at the moment while you gave her another pair of shoes to wear inside the house. "Where are the others? " "…. They are upstairs, setting the most iMpOrTaNt room. " Instantly understanding what you meant, your mother and you both started laughing. "Literally, its like he never ever got a room for himself…. He's so happy right now. " "He's a cute kid, just like you. I still remember how much you were jumping around like a monkey after knowing you got your own room. " "Mommm~~ stop calling me a monkey. " laughing she grasped your chin gently and began to caress it lovingly. "At least you are my monkey, my cute monkey. " "… I love you so much Mom. " Again you hugged her dearly then took her hand after breaking the hug and pulled her towards the stairs. "Com'on, let's see what they are doing. "

Opening the door, you saw them engrossed in their work. " Look who's finally here! " Gasping hard "NANNYYYY~~" Your son ran and engulfed her legs as tight as he could. And so did your mother, picked him up and hugged him tight. "Look nanny, my room. Isn't it super good? Daddy and grandpa set it. " your mother gasped dramatically to satisfy her cutie pie "My God, this is so beautiful… Awe finally my cutie is big enough to stay alone in his own room, *she moved and kissed the crown of his head* I'm so proud of you! " That was enough to make his soft self giggle cutely. "Welcome mother! " Your dear husband moved further and hugged her close. "I should be the one to welcome you all dear.. I came here to work with you guys but I guess, you didn't leave anything for me. And this house.... You set it so beautifully Jungkook. " " Thank you sooo much mother. "

"Dear, you didn't bring the sweet? " Your father, who was standing there the whole time, seeing his wife so happy with their only dear daughter and her family spoke up. "Ah.. Oops-sorry. Actually, I was busy in making these so I got late in helping you guys with work. Here I got these for you all. Congratulations for your new sweet home! " "Mom... you didn't have to~. " Your eyes moved towards jungkook, seeing him stare back at you with the adoration and love, he was holding for your mother, well his as well. Looking back at your mother, jungkook held the bag of pastries and you finally hugged your mother again. This time with a thanking heart towards God. He is indeed the most merciful, blessing you with such a pure mother figure that you wouldn't ever trade for anything in the world.

"You are the best. " "My baby~" Turning her head to the side, she kissed your temple and rubbed your back smoothly. "Wish I listened to you that time..... We wouldn't have to go through all that-" "Don't!.. Let's just forget it all. Behave as if it didn't happen ever in your lives. It was written in fate and you guys were OBLIGED to face it all. So don't say like you were at fault and now you regret it deeply. At least you both's love is more stronger now... Also that incident made you believe just how many hurdles will come, if YOU both are together..... then nothing can set you apart. So accept what fate brings to you and learn to live with the flow.... This is what life is! " " Mommy what happened at that time? " "uh.. "

Looking at your husband who started off with something evil in his mind cause of course, his expressions said it all.

"Let's just say, when your mommy was angry with me, I brought a small baby at home so that she could forgive me. And guess what,

your mommy was so happy by your arrival that she did actually forgave me. " Laughing at his dumb statement, you went near him and hugged him all tight, who hugged you back as tightly as he could along with you both's cute bundle of joy as well.

"This was it. What I ever longed for. And finally after getting what I wanted... I could never be more thankful. Knowing how tough my life was at some point, I could never forget that accident, which changed our lives, our whole relationship, the whole me.... I could never thank Father David and Mr. Wang any less. Just if he was one more minute late I-... I would have been dead at this time. It was such a miracle that the soul hadn't get Jungkook's body at that time, so it was all fruitful at the end..... "   " So you believe in bad soul and curse now? " ".... Obviously! I think a curse can be broken..... But it does leave some scars behind. Like the scar on my neck.... And the nightmares I still get every night.... I still feel like there's something around me...either when I'm alone or with my family.. I still feel some things..at day or night.... Guess they are totally right...
A curse can be broken, but it will never Die!!